Favorite Fairy Tales

TOLD IN SCOTLAND

Favorite Fairy Tales

TOLD IN SCOTLAND

Retold
by
VIRGINIA HAVILAND
Illustrated
by
ADRIENNE ADAMS

Boston   LITTLE, BROWN AND COMPANY   Toronto

These stories have been retold from the following sources:

THE PAGE BOY AND THE SILVER GOBLET, THE BROWNIE O' FERNE-
DEN, and PEERIFOOL, from SCOTTISH FAIRY TALES by Elizabeth
W. Grierson (New York, Stokes, 1910).

THE WEE BANNOCK, from MORE ENGLISH FAIRY TALES by Joseph
Jacobs (New York, G. P. Putnam's Sons, 1894).

THE GOOD HOUSEWIFE AND HER NIGHT LABORS, from CHILDREN'S
BOOK OF CELTIC STORIES (London, Black, 1908).

ASSIPATTLE AND THE GIANT SEA SERPENT, from SCOTTISH FAIRY
AND FOLK TALES by Sir George Douglas (London, Scott, 1894;
New York, Scribner, 1894).

*Published simultaneously in Canada
by Little, Brown & Company (Canada) Limited*

PRINTED IN THE UNITED STATES OF AMERICA

Contents

The Page Boy and
the Silver Goblet

THERE WAS ONCE a little page boy who was in service at a great castle in Scotland. He was a good-natured lad and performed his duties willingly and well. Everyone liked him, from the grand laird whom he served to the fat old steward whose errands he ran.

The castle stood on the edge of a high cliff overlooking the sea. The castle walls were very thick, but in them on one side was cut a special little door. It opened on a narrow flight of steps that led down the face of the cliff to the shore. Anyone who liked could go down there on pleasant summer days to bathe in the shimmering sea.

On the other side of the castle, gardens and pleasure grounds opened onto a long stretch of moor. This moorland, covered with purple heather, met in the distance a range of stony hills.

The little page boy liked to run out to the moor when his work was done, for here he could catch butterflies and look for birds' nests when it was nesting time.

The old steward himself was glad to have the lad play there. But before the boy went out, the old man always warned him:

"Now, mind my words, laddie, and keep far away from the Fairy Knowe, for you cannot trust the Little Folk."

This Knowe was a rocky green hillock, which stood on the moor not twenty yards from the garden gate. People said that it was the home of fairies. And everyone knew that the fairies would punish any rash mortal who came too near them. Because of this the country folk would walk a good half-mile out of their way, even in daylight, to avoid going too near the Fairy Knowe. At night they would hardly step on the moor; for then, as everyone knows, the fairies come abroad in the darkness. And they leave the door of their dwelling open, so that an unlucky mortal who does not take care may find himself inside.

Now the little page boy, instead of being frightened of the fairies, was anxious to see them. He wanted to visit their home, just to find out what it was like.

One night, when everyone else was asleep, he crept out of the castle by the little side door. He stole down the stone steps and along the shore. Up on the moor, he went straight to the Fairy Knowe.

To his delight he found that what everyone said was true. The top of the rocky Knowe was tipped up, and from this opening rays of light streamed out.

His heart beat fast with excitement as, gathering his courage, he stooped down and slipped inside the Knowe.

He found himself in a large room lit by hundreds of tiny candles. Around a polished table sat scores of the Little People. They were dressed in green, and yellow, and pink; in blue, and lilac, and scarlet — in all the colors possible.

The page boy stood in a dark corner watching, in wonder, a busy scene of feasting. How strange that here, within sight of the castle, all these tiny beings were living their lives unknown to men!

Suddenly someone gave an order.

"Fetch the cup!" cried a shrill voice. Instantly two fairy pages, in scarlet livery, darted from the table to a tiny cupboard in the rock. They returned staggering under the weight of a beautiful silver cup. Richly embossed it was, and lined with shining gold.

Up to the middle of the table they lifted the cup. Then, with clapping of hands and shouts of

joy, all the fairies began in turn to drink from it.

The page boy could see, from where he stood, that although no one poured wine into the goblet it was always full. Also, he saw that the drink was not always of the same kind. Each fairy, when he grasped the goblet's stem, wished for the drink that he loved best; and lo! in a moment the cup became full.

It would be a fine thing if I could show that cup at the castle, thought the page boy. No one will believe that I have been here unless I have something to show for it. He bided his time and watched.

Presently the fairies noticed the page boy. Instead of being angry at him for entering their dwelling, as he had expected they would be, they seemed pleased to see him. They even invited him to a seat at their feast.

Later, however, they became rude. They jeered at him for being content to serve mere mortals, and told him that they saw everything that went on at the castle. They made fun of the fat old steward, whom the page boy loved with all his heart. They laughed at the castle food, saying that it was fit only for animals. When the scarlet-clad pages set a fresh dainty on their table, the fairies pushed the dish across to the boy, saying, "Taste this, for you cannot eat such things at the castle."

At last the page boy could stand their teasing no longer. Besides, he knew that if he wanted to secure the cup he must lose no time.

Suddenly he stood up. Tightly he grasped the stem of the silver goblet. "I'll drink to you all in water," he cried. Instantly, the ruby wine was turned to clear cold water.

He raised the cup to his lips, but he did not drink from it. With a sudden jerk he threw the water over the candles. Instantly the room was in darkness. Clasping the precious cup tightly in his arms, he sprang to the opening of the Knowe, through which he could see the stars glimmering.

Soon the page boy was speeding over the wet, dew-spangled moor, with the whole troop of fairies at his heels. They were wild with rage and uttered shrill shouts of fury. The page boy knew well that, if they should overtake him, he would have no mercy at their hands.

His heart began to sink, for, fleet of foot

though he was, he was no match for the Little Folk. They gained on him steadily.

All seemed lost, when a strange voice sounded out of the darkness:

"*If thou wouldst gain the castle door,
Keep to the black stones on the shore.*"

It was the voice of some poor mortal who had been taken by the fairies and who did not want a like fate to befall the brave page boy.

This made the page boy remember a saying he had heard: *He who walks on wet sands, which the waves have washed, the fairies cannot touch.*

The page boy turned, and dashed, panting, down to the shore. At first, his feet sank in dry sand. His breath came in little gasps, and he felt as if he must give up his struggle. But he pushed on; and at last, just as the first of the fairies was about to lay hands on him, he made a long jump. He landed on wet sand from which the waves had just receded, and he knew that he was safe.

The Little Folk could go not one step farther. They had to remain on the dry sand, shrieking with cries of rage and disappointment.

The triumphant page boy ran safely along the shore, with the precious cup in his arms. He climbed lightly up the steps in the rock, and disappeared through the little door.

For many years, long after the page boy had grown up and become a stately steward who trained other page boys, the beautiful cup remained in the castle. It was a witness to his adventure in outwitting the fairies.

The Wee Bannock

ONCE UPON A TIME in Scotland an old man
and an old woman lived in a wee cottage. They
were contented enough, for besides their cottage
and their garden, they had two cows, five hens and
a cock, a cat and two kittens.

The old man looked after the cows, and the
hens, and the garden. The old woman kept busy
spinning. The kittens often jumped at her spindle,
and she would say: "Sho, sho! Go away!"

One day after breakfast the old woman thought

she would make a bannock for their evening meal. She put her griddle over the fire, and baked two fine oatmeal cakes. When they were done she set them before the fire to harden.

As the bannocks were toasting, the goodwife's husband came in from the barn. He sat down beside the fire to rest in his great chair. After a while, his eyes spied the bannocks. He took one and snapped it through the middle. Then he began to eat it.

When the other bannock saw this, it up and ran across the kitchen and out the door as fast as it could roll. The old woman started after it, with her spindle in one hand and her distaff in the other.

But the wee bannock ran faster than she did, and it escaped over the hill behind the cottage. It ran, and it ran, and it ran, until it came to a big thatched house. Here it went boldly in, and over to the fireside.

Now it happened that this house belonged to a tailor. He and his two apprentices were sitting

cross-legged on a big table, sewing away with all their might.

When they saw the wee bannock come rolling across the floor, all three got such a fright that they jumped down from their table and hid behind the tailor's goodwife, who was carding away by the fire.

Up she jumped with her carding, and the tailor up, too, with his ironing goose. One apprentice grasped the shears and the other the ironing board. All of them tried to catch the wee bannock. But the bannock dodged them all and ran round about the fire. One of the lads, thinking to snip it with the shears, fell into the ashes. The bannock at last got out the door, with the tailor throwing the ironing goose at it and the goodwife her carding tools.

The bannock ran too quickly for them, however. On and on it rolled until it came to a wee cottage by the road. In here it ran and found a weaver sitting at his loom. The weaver's wife sat beside him, winding a hank of yarn.

"What's that, Tibby?" asked the weaver, as the little cake rolled past him.

"Oh," she cried in delight, " 'tis a wee bannock!

Aye, and it's well come. Our porridge was but thin today."

"Grip it, woman, grip it," called her husband.

"Aye, but that's a clever bannock. Catch it, Willie! Catch it, man!"

"Hoot," answered Willie. "Throw your wool at it now!"

But it was in vain that the goodwife threw her wool at it and that the weaver tried to corner it and knock it down with his shuttle. The wee bannock dodged and it turned and it twisted till at last it flew right out at the door again.

Over the hill it went, like a mad cow.

On and on it ran, to another house, and again in, to the fireplace.

This time the wee bannock found the goodwife in her kitchen, churning. When she spied the wee bannock, she cried out: "Come now, wee cake! 'Tis bannock and cream I'll have for my dinner this day."

But the wee bannock dodged about the churn,

and the goodwife after it. In such a hurry she was that she all but upset her churn. And before she got it set right again, the wee bannock was off and down the hill to the mill. And in it ran.

The miller was sifting meal, but he looked up at the wee bannock as it rolled across the floor.

"Aye, 'tis a sign of plenty, just, when bannocks are running about and nobody to look after them. But I like bannock and cheese. Come your way hither now, and I'll give you a night's quarters, Wee Bannock."

But the little bannock was not going to trust itself to the miller and his cheese. So it turned fast and ran right out again. The miller was that busy that he did not chase it, either.

The wee bannock toddled away and on and on, till it came to the smithy, and in it popped, and right up to the anvil.

The smith was at work making horse nails when the wee bannock entered.

"Aye, I do like a glass of good ale and a well-

toasted bannock," he cried. "Come your way in by here."

But the wee bannock was afraid when it heard about the ale. It turned and was off, as hard as it could go, and the smith after it with his hammer. When the smith saw that he could not catch up to it, he flung his heavy hammer after it, to knock it down. But, luckily for the wee bannock, he missed and the bannock was now out of sight.

On and on ran the bannock till it came to a farmhouse with a great stack of peats drying for the fire. Into the house it ran and up to the fireside. Here the goodman was working with flax, separating the lint from the stalks with a cloving stick. His goodwife was combing what he had already separated.

"Oh, Janet!" cried the goodman. "Here's a wee bannock come in. It looks that good — I'll have a half of it."

"Well, John, and I'll have the other half," cried the goodwife. "Hit it over the back with your stick, or it will be out at the door again," she said.

But the bannock was clever and played catch-me-if-you-can.

"Hoot, toot!" cried Janet when she saw her husband miss it. And she threw her tool at it, too. But it was far too clever to be hit.

This time the wee bannock ran along the brook till it came to a wee cottage standing in the heather.

Here the goodwife was stirring the soup. Her goodman was braiding straw ropes for tying the cows.

"Oh, Jock! Come, here, come!" cried the good-wife. "You are forever crying for a wee bannock for the supper. Here is one come right through our door. Quick, and I'll help you grip it."

"Aye, Mother. But where is it?"

"See there, man, there, under the chair," cried his wife. "Run over to that side; I'll keep to this."

But the bannock ran behind Jock's chair and

Jock, in his haste, tripped and fell. The wee clever bannock jumped over him and flew out the door.

Through the bushes of gorse it ran, and over the hill, and down to a shepherd's cottage. In it rolled and snug to the fireside.

The folk here were just sitting down to their porridge, and the goodwife was scraping out the pot for all the wee bairns at the table.

"Well now," she exclaimed, with her spoon in the air. "Here's a wee bannock come in to warm itself at our fireside."

"Shut the door," cried her husband, "and we'll try to get a grip on it. It would come in handy after our porridge."

When the bannock heard that, it did not wait for the door to be closed. It whirled away and ran off as fast as it could, with the shepherd and his goodwife and all their wee bairns after it.

The shepherd threw his bonnet after the bannock. But it escaped and rolled on to another house. Here the folk were just going to bed.

The goodman had just stepped out of his breeks,
and the goodwife was raking the fire.

"What's that?" asked he.

"Oh, it's a wee bannock!" she said.

"Grip it! I could eat the half of it," said he.

"Catch it, then," answered his wife, "and I'll

have a bit, too. Quick! Quick! Cast your breeks at it, or it will be away."

The goodman threw his breeks on the little bannock and nearly smothered it. But it wriggled out bravely, and ran into the dark of evening. The goodman went on and on, chasing the wee bannock, far across the moor; but then he lost it.

As for the poor wee bannock, it thought it had better creep under a gorse bush and lie there till morning. But it was so dark that it could not see a fox's hole that was there. Down it fell, into it; and the fox very glad to see it, just, for he had got no food for two days.

"Oh, welcome, welcome," said the fox. And he snapped it through the middle, and that was the end of the poor wee bannock.

Peerifool

ONCE UPON A TIME in Scotland there were
a King and a Queen who had three daughters.
When the Princesses were just growing into young
women, the King died. The crown went to a dis-
tant cousin, who had always hated the old King.
As the new King, he paid no heed to the poor
widowed Queen and her daughters.

Being poor now, the Queen and the Princesses
had to live in a tiny cottage and do all the housework themselves. In a garden in front of the cot-

tage they grew cabbages. In a small field behind the cottage they kept a cow, to whom they fed the cabbages so that she would give them more milk.

But they soon discovered that someone was coming at night and stealing their cabbages. This vexed them, because they knew that if they did not feed cabbages to the cow she would not give them enough milk to sell.

One day the eldest Princess said she would sit in the garden all night to see if she could catch the thief. She took out a three-legged stool and wrapped herself in a blanket, to spend the night in the cold and the dark.

At first it seemed as if all her trouble would be in vain. Hour after hour passed with nothing happening. But just as the clock was striking two, she heard a trampling in the field behind, as if some heavy person were trying to tread softly. Soon a mighty giant stepped right over the wall into the garden.

The giant carried an enormous creel on his arm,

and a long sharp knife in his hand. He began to
cut the cabbages, and as fast as he could he tossed
them into the basket.

Now, the Princess was no coward; although she
had not expected to face a giant, she gathered up
her courage and cried out sharply: "Who gave

you liberty to cut our cabbages? Leave off this minute, and go away!"

The giant paid no heed, but went on steadily cutting and tossing.

"Do you not hear me?" the Princess cried out in fury. She had been the Princess Royal, and she was accustomed to being obeyed.

"If you be not quiet, I will take you too," said the giant grimly, pressing the cabbages down into the creel.

"I should like to see you try," retorted the Princess. She rose from her stool and stamped her foot. In her anger, she forgot that she was only a weak lass and that he was a powerful giant.

As if to show how strong he was, the giant suddenly seized her by her arm and her leg. He put her in his creel on top of the cabbages, and off they went.

When he reached his great house, which was on a lonely moor, he took her out, and set her down roughly.

"Now you will be my servant," he said. "You will keep my house, and do my errands. Every day you must drive my cow to the hillside. And see this bag of wool? After you have taken the cow to pasture, you must come back and settle yourself at home, as a good housewife should, to comb and card and spin this wool into yarn. You will then weave the yarn into good thick cloth for my garments. When I come home I shall expect to find all this done, and a great pot of porridge ready for my supper."

The poor Princess was dismayed when she heard these words. She had not been used to working hard, and there had always been her sisters to help her. The giant took no notice of her distress, but went out as soon as it was daylight, leaving her alone in the house to begin her work.

As soon as he had gone she drove the cow to the pasture, as he had told her to do. It was a long walk over the moor and by the time she was back at the house again she felt very tired.

She thought that she would put on the pot and boil herself some porridge before she began to card and comb the wool. Just as she was sitting down to the porridge, the door opened. In trooped a crowd of wee fairies — the Peerie Folk.

These were the tiniest men and women the Princess had ever seen. Not one of them would have reached halfway to her knee. They were dressed in all the colors of the rainbow — scarlet and blue, green and yellow, orange and violet; and every one of them had a shock of yellow hair.

Their talking and laughing filled the room. First they hopped up onto the stools, then onto the chairs. Finally, they reached the table top and

clustered around the Princess's bowl of porridge.

"We be hungry, we be hungry," they cried, in tiny shrill voices. "Spare a little porridge for the Peerie Folk."

But the Princess was hungry also. And, besides being hungry, she was tired and cross and not at all comfortable with the Peerie Folk staring at her. She shook her head and impatiently waved them away with her spoon, saying sharply:

"Little for one, and less for two,
And never a grain have I for you."

To her great delight the Peerie Folk vanished at once.

Now she finished her porridge in peace. She took the wool out of the bag, and set to work to comb and card it. But it seemed as if it were bewitched. It curled and twisted and coiled itself round her fingers. Try as she would, she could not do anything with it.

When the giant came home he found the Princess sitting in despair with confusion all around her. The porridge which she had left for him had burned to a cinder.

Well, now, the giant was angry, just. He raged, and stamped, and cried out the most dreadful words. At last he took the Princess by the heels and beat her until her back was skinned and bleeding. Then he carried her out to his byre and threw her up among the hens. She was so stunned and bruised that she could only lie there, looking down on the backs of the cows.

Time went on, and in the garden at home the cabbages disappeared as fast as ever. The second Princess now said that she would do as her sister had done. She would wrap herself in a blanket, and sit all night on a stool in the garden to see what was happening.

Exactly the same fate befell the second Princess as had befallen her sister. The giant appeared with his creel and carried her off. He set her to mind the cow and the house, and to make his porridge and to spin. Again the little yellow-headed Peerie Folk appeared and asked for some supper. She, also, refused to give any porridge to them. After that, she, too, could not comb or card her wool. And the giant was just as angry this time. He scolded her, and beat her, and threw her up beside her sister to lie among the hens.

The youngest Princess next determined to sit in the garden all night. She wanted now not so much to see what was becoming of the cabbages, as to discover what had happened to her sisters.

When the giant came and carried her off, she was not at all sorry. Rather, she was glad, for she was a brave and loving little lassie. She felt that now she had a chance to find out whether her sisters were dead or alive.

Lying in the creel, she was even cheerful. She felt certain that she was quite clever enough to outwit the giant, if only she remained watchful and patient. So she lay quite quietly on the cabbages, keeping her eyes wide open to see by which road he carried her off.

At his home he set her down in his kitchen, and told her all that he expected her to do. But, unlike her sisters, she was not dismayed. She nodded her head brightly, and said that she felt sure that she could do it all.

She sang to herself as she drove the cow over the moor to pasture. She ran the whole way back, so that she would have a long afternoon to work at the wool. Also, although she had not told the giant this, she was going to search through his house.

Before she set to work, she made some porridge, just as her sisters had done. As she was about to sup it, the little Peerie Folk trooped in. They climbed up on the table, and stood and stared at her.

"We be hungry, we be hungry," they cried. "Spare a little porridge for the Peerie Folk."

"With all my heart," replied the kind Princess. "If you can find dishes small enough for you to sup out of, I will fill them for you. If I were to give you bowls like mine, you would drown yourselves in the porridge."

At these words, the Peerie Folk squealed with laughter till their straw-colored hair tumbled over their faces. They hopped to the floor and ran out of the house. Soon they trooped back. In their wee hands they carried cups of bluebells and foxgloves, and saucers of primroses and anemones.

The Princess poured a tiny spoonful of porridge into each saucer and a drop of milk into each cup. With neat little grass spoons, which they drew from their pockets, the Peerie Folk ate it all up daintily and quickly.

When they had finished they all cried out, "Thank you! Thank you!" and ran out of the kitchen again, leaving the Princess alone. And now alone, she searched the house for her sisters, but, of course, she could not find them.

Never mind, I will find them soon, she said to herself. Tomorrow I will search among the cows and chickens in the byre. In the meantime, I had better get on with my work. . . . Back to the kitchen she went, and took out the bag of wool, which the giant had ordered her to make into cloth.

Just as she began working on the wool, the door opened once again and a yellow-haired Peerie Boy entered. He was like the other Peerie Folk, but bigger, and he wore a rich suit of grass-green velvet. Boldly he walked to the middle of the kitchen and looked around.

"Hast thou any work for me to do?" he asked. "I ken well how to handle wool and turn it into fine thick cloth."

"I have plenty of work," replied the Princess, "but I have no money to pay for it."

"All the wages that I ask is that thou wilt take the trouble to find out my name. Few folk ken it, and few folk care to ken. But if by any chance thou canst not find it out, then must thou pay toll of half thy cloth."

The Princess thought that it would be quite an easy thing to find out the Peerie Boy's name, so she agreed to the bargain. Putting all the wool back into the bag, she handed it to him. He swung it over his shoulder and off he skipped.

The Princess ran to the door to notice which way he went, for she had made up her mind that she would follow him secretly to his home. She would learn his name from his neighbors.

To her great dismay, she saw that he had vanished completely. She began to wonder what would happen when the giant came back and found that she had allowed some nameless person to carry off the wool.

The afternoon wore on, and she had thought of no way to learn who the boy was, or where he came from. She began to be frightened.

In the gloaming, as the sun was beginning to set, a knock came at the door. When she opened it, she found an old woman who begged for a night's lodging.

The Princess was so kindhearted she wanted to grant the poor dame's request, but she feared what the giant would say. She explained that she could not take her in for the night, as she was only a servant, and not the mistress of the house. However, she seated her and gave her bread and milk. Also, she brought her water in which to bathe her poor, tired feet.

The Princess was so bonny and gentle and kind

that the old woman gave her her blessing, and told her not to vex herself — as it was a fine, dry night, and she had had a meal, she could easily sleep in the shelter of the byre.

Strange to say, as the old woman lay down there, she felt the earth beneath her grow warmer and warmer. Finally, it roasted her so that she had to crawl up the side of the hillock behind the byre to get fresh air.

As she neared the top of the hillock, she heard a voice beneath her saying: "TEASE, TEASENS, TEASE; CARD, CARDENS, CARD; SPIN, SPINNENS, SPIN; FOR PEERIFOOL, PEERIFOOL, PEERIFOOL IS WHAT MEN CALL ME."

When the old woman got to the very top, she found a crack in the earth through which rays of

light shone forth. She put her eye to the crack, and what should she see down below her but a brilliantly lighted chamber. Here all the Peerie Folk sat in a circle, working away as hard as they could.

Some of them were carding wool, some were combing it, others were spinning it, constantly wetting their fingers with their lips, in order to twist the yarn fine. Some were spinning the yarn into cloth.

Round and round the circle, cracking a little whip, and urging them to work faster, was a yellow-haired Peerie Boy.

"This be a strange thing, and these be queer goings-on," said the old woman to herself, creeping hastily down the hillock. "I must go and tell the bonny lassie in the house yonder. Maybe knowing what I have seen will stand her in good stead some day. When there be Peerie Folk about, it is well to be on guard."

Back to the house she went and told the Princess all that she had seen and heard. The Princess was so delighted that now she risked the giant's wrath and allowed the woman to go and sleep in the hayloft.

Not long after, the door opened. It was the Peerie Boy once more, with webs of cloth upon his shoulder. "Here is thy cloth," he said, with a sly smile. "I will put it on the shelf for thee the moment that thou tellest me what my name is."

The Princess, who was a merry maiden, thought that she would tease the little fellow for a time before letting him know that she had found out his secret.

She called out first one name and then another, always pretending to think that she had hit upon the right one. And all the time the Peerie Boy jumped from side to side with delight. She would never find the right name, so half of the cloth would be his.

At last the Princess grew tired of joking, and she cried out with a laugh: "Dost thou by any chance ken anyone called PEERIFOOL?"

The Peerie Boy was now so angry and disappointed that he flung the webs of cloth down in a heap on the floor and ran away, slamming the door behind him.

Just now, at dusk, the giant was coming down the hill. To his astonishment, he met a troop of Peerie Folk toiling up it, so tired that they could hardly move. Their eyes were dim, their heads were hanging, and their lips were so long and twisted that the poor little folk looked quite hideous.

The giant asked what was troubling them. They answered that they had had to spin the day long for their master until they were quite exhausted. The reason why their lips were pulled down so long was that they had used them all day to wet their fingers, so that they might make a fine thread.

"I have always admired women who could spin," said the giant, "and I have looked for a housewife that could do so. Now, after this, I will

be more careful, for my housewife is a bonny little woman. I would not have her spoil her face."

He hurried home, afraid that he would find his new servant's pretty red lips had grown long and ugly in his absence.

Great was his relief to see the lassie standing by the table, bonny as ever, with all the webs of cloth in a pile before her.

"By my troth, thou art an industrious maiden," he said, in high good humor. "As a reward for working so diligently, I will restore thy sisters to thee." Out he went to the byre, to bring back the other two Princesses.

Their little sister nearly screamed aloud when she saw how ill they looked. But, wisely, she held her tongue and busied herself with rubbing a cooling ointment on their wounds and binding them up.

When her sisters had revived again and the giant had gone to bed, they told her all that had befallen them.

"I shall avenge his cruelty," said the little Princess firmly.

Next morning, before the giant was up, the little Princess fetched his creel and put her eldest sister into it. She covered her with fine silken hangings and tapestries, and on the top put handfuls of grass. When the giant came down to breakfast, she asked him, in her sweetest voice, if he would do her a favor.

The giant, of course, was very pleased with her because of the quality of cloth which he thought she had spun. He answered that he would gladly do her a favor.

"Then I want you to carry that creelful of grass home for my mother's cow," said the Princess. "It will help to make up for all the cabbages you have stolen from her garden."

Wonderful to relate, the giant did as he was bid and carried the creel to the cottage.

Next morning, the youngest Princess put her second sister into a creel. She covered her with

pieces of fine linen and topped it all with an armful of grass. At her bidding the giant, who was by
now very fond of his housekeeper, carried this
creel also home to her mother.

The next day, the little Princess told the giant
that she thought she would go for a long walk
after she had done her housework. She might not
be in when he came home at night, but she would
have another creelful of grass ready for him to
carry to the cottage. He promised to do so. Then,
as usual, he went out for the day.

In the afternoon, the clever little lassie went
through the house, gathering together all the lace,
and silver, and jewelry that she could find. She
placed them beside a creel. She cut an armful of
grass next and laid it down beside them.

Now she crept into the creel herself, and pulled
all the fine things in around and above her. She
covered everything with the grass — and a very
difficult thing to do it was, with herself at the
bottom of the basket. She then lay quite still and
waited.

Presently the giant came along, and, as he promised, lifted the creel and carried it off to the Queen's cottage.

When he arrived at the cottage, no one seemed to be at home, so he set down the creel and turned to go away. But the little Princess had told her sisters exactly what to do when he arrived. They had a great can of boiling water ready upstairs. When they heard him coming around the house, they emptied it over his head. And that was the end of the giant!

The Brownie o' Ferne-Den

MANY BROWNIES there have been in Scotland. And one of them was known as "the Brownie o' Ferne-Den."

Now Ferne-Den was a farmhouse. It had its name from the glen, or "den," near which it stood, for anyone who wished to reach the farm had to pass through this glen.

All around, the country folk believed that a brownie lived in the glen. Never would he appear to anyone in the daytime, but it was said he was sometimes seen at night. He would steal about like an ungainly shadow, moving from tree to tree to keep from being seen. And he never did harm to anybody, this Brownie o' Ferne-Den.

Indeed, like all good brownies that are properly treated and let alone, the Brownie o' Ferne-Den was always on the lookout to do a good turn to those in need of his help.

The farmer of Ferne-Den did not know what he would ever do without this brownie. If he had any farmwork to be finished in a hurry, it would be done. The brownie would thrash his grain, and winnow it, and tie it up into bags. He would cut the turnips, too. And for the farmer's wife he would wash the clothes, work the churn, or weed the garden.

All that the farmer and his wife had to do was to leave open the door of the barn, or the turnip shed, or the milkhouse, when they went to bed. And they must put down a bowl of new milk on the doorstep for the brownie's supper. When they woke the next morning the bowl would be empty, and the job would be finished better than if it had been done by mortal hands.

Now all of this should have proved how gentle and kindly this brownie was. But all the workers on the farm had a fear of him. They would go miles around in the dark, coming home from kirk on the Sunday or market on Market Day, to avoid passing through the brownie's glen and catching a sight of him.

The farmer's lady herself was so good and gentle a housewife that she felt no fear of the brownie. When the brownie's supper was to be left outside, it was she who would fill his bowl with the richest milk, and she would add a good spoonful of cream to it, too.

"Aye," said she, "he works hard for us, right enough, and never asks for wages. Well does he deserve the very best meal we can set out for him."

One night this gentle lady was taken ill, and

everyone was afraid she might die. Her husband
took it hard, indeed, and so, too, did her servants.
Such a good mistress she had ever been to them
that they loved her as if she were their mother.
Now she was that bad that they were all for send-
ing for the old nurse who lived miles off on the
other side of the glen.

Who was to go to fetch her? That was the question. It was black midnight when the lady fell ill,
and the only way to the old nurse's house lay
straight through the glen. Whoever traveled that
road would run the risk of meeting the brownie.

The farmer himself would have gone, well
enough, but he dared not leave his wife. As for the
timid servants, they stood about in the kitchen,
each telling the other that he was the one to go.
And no one of them offered to go himself.

Little did they know that the brownie, who
was the very cause of their fear, was hiding only
a few feet away from them, in the entry outside
the kitchen. There he crouched, a queer wee man,

all covered with hair. He had a long beard and red-rimmed eyes. His broad feet were webbed like those of a duck, and his long arms touched the ground, even when he stood up.

The brownie, with his face all anxious, tried to hear their words. He had come as usual from his home in the glen to see if there were any work for him to do, and to look for his bowl of milk. He knew fine that something now was wrong inside the farmhouse. Usually, at this late hour, all was dark and still, but here were the windows lit up and the door wide open.

The brownie learned from the servants' jabber that his kind mistress, whom he loved so dearly, was deathly ill. He became sad, indeed. And when he found that the silly servants were so full of their fears that they dared not go for the nurse, his anger grew far greater than their fear.

"Fools and idiots!" he muttered, stamping his queer flat feet. "They talk as if a brownie would take a bite right off them. If the like of them only knew the bother they give me to keep out of *their* way, they would not be so silly. Aye, by my troth, if they keep on like this, the bonny lady will die amongst their fingers. It strikes me that brownie must away, himself, for the nurse."

Up he reached with his hand and took down from its peg on the wall the farmer's great dark cloak. Hiding under it, he hurried out to the stable, to saddle and bridle the farmer's fleetest horse.

When the last buckle was fastened, the brownie led the horse out of the stable and scrambled up onto its back. "If ever you have flown fast, fly fast now," begged the brownie.

It was as if the horse understood the brownie. It gave a quick whinny, pricked up its ears, and darted into the darkness like an arrow from a bow.

In less time than the distance had ever been traveled before, the brownie came to the old woman's cottage.

Now the nurse, of course, was in bed asleep.

The brownie had to rap sharply on her window. When she rose and put her old face close to the glass to ask who was there, he told her quickly why he had come at this late hour.

"You must come with me, Goodwife, and that at once," he commanded in a deep voice, "if the lady of Ferne-Den is to be saved. There is no one to nurse her at the farm save the lot of silly servants."

"Aye, but how shall I get there? Have they sent a cart for me?" asked the old woman. As far as she could see, there was nothing at the door save the horse and its rider.

"Nay, they have sent no cart," replied the brownie. "You must just climb up behind me on the saddle, and hang on tight. I'll promise to land you at Ferne-Den safe and sound."

The brownie's voice was so commanding that the old woman dared not refuse to do as she was bid. Besides, she had often ridden thus on a horse when she was a lassie. So, she made haste to dress herself and soon unlocked her door. She climbed up behind the stranger, who was almost hidden in his dark cloak. She clasped him tightly and they were off.

Not a word was spoken between them till they neared the glen. Then the old woman began to feel her courage giving way. "Do you think we might meet the brownie?" she asked timidly. "I have no fancy to run the risk, for folk say that he is an unchancy creature."

The brownie gave his own odd laugh. "Keep up your heart, and cease talking foolishly," he said. "I promise you there will be naught uglier this night than the man you ride behind."

"Oh, good on you, then, I'm fine and safe," said the old woman. "I have not seen your face, but I warrant you are a true man, for the care you have taken of the poor lady of Ferne-Den."

She fell into silence again till they had passed through the glen and the good horse had turned into the farmyard. The brownie now slid to the ground. Turning around, he carefully lifted her down with his long, strong arms. But — as he did so, the cloak slipped off him. She saw his strange, short body.

"In all the world, what kind of man are you?" the old woman asked. She peered into his face in the graying light of morning. "What makes your eyes so big? And what have you done to your feet? They are more like duck's webs than aught else."

The queer little brownie laughed. "I've walked many a mile without a horse to help me, and I've heard it said that too much walking makes the feet unshapely.

"But waste no time in talking now, good dame. Go into the house. And if anyone asks who brought you hither so quickly, tell them — they who fear the brownie — that there was a lack of men to help the good mistress. You had to ride here behind the BROWNIE O' FERNE-DEN."

The Good Housewife and Her Night Labors

ONCE UPON A TIME there was in Scotland a farmer who had a very thrifty wife. She was so thrifty that she would gather the little bits of wool that grazing sheep left here and there on the moorland and bring them to her cottage. After her family had gone to bed, the goodwife, whose name was Inary, sat up late, carding the wool and spinning it into yarn. Then she would weave the yarn into warm cloth, to make garments for her children.

With all this late work, Inary became weary. One night, sitting at her loom, she was so tired that she lay down her shuttle, buried her head in her hands, and burst out weeping.

"Oh, if only someone would come, from near or far, from land or sea, to help make my cloth," she sobbed.

No sooner had the words left her lips than she heard a knocking on her door.

"Who is there?" she cried, placing her ear to the keyhole.

"Inary, good housewife, open your door to me. As long as I have, you'll get," spoke a strange voice.

Inary hesitated, but then she opened the door. There on the threshold stood an odd, wee woman, dressed all in green, with a white cap on her head.

In her astonishment, Inary only stood and stared. But the wee visitor, without another word, ran straight to the spinning wheel and began to make it whir.

The goodwife shut the door and turned away. Then she heard another knock, even louder. When she asked who was there, a shrill voice repeated the same strange words she had heard before: "Inary, good housewife, open your door to me. As long as I have, you'll get."

When Inary opened the door this time she saw another queer, wee woman standing on the threshold.

This creature, too, ran into the house without waiting to say by-your-leave. She sat herself at the loom and began to throw the weaving shuttle back and forth.

Before the goodwife could shut her door this time, a funny little man in green trousers came out of the darkness. He seized hold of a handful of wool and began to card it. Another wee woman followed him, and then another, and another, until it seemed to the good housewife that all the fairies and pixies in Scotland were entering her house.

The kitchen was alive with eager, busy fairies. Some of them were hanging the great pot on the fire to boil the fulling water for washing the dirty wool. Some were combing and untangling the clean wool. Others were spinning it into yarn, and plying the shuttle to weave the yarn into great webs of cloth.

The din and rattle of their work was like to deafen the good housewife, and to awaken her husband who was sleeping away as if under a spell. *Splash-splash! Whirr-whirr! Clack-clack!* . . . The water in the pot bubbled over. The spinning wheel whirred round and round. The shuttle flew backwards and forwards in the loom. . . . It seemed as if Inary would be deafened by the clatter!

The worst of the noise was their shrill crying for something to eat. The goodwife put on her griddle and baked bannocks as fast as she could. But the bannocks were eaten up the moment they came off the fire, and the visitors shouted for more and more.

Good Inary became far more tired than she had been to begin with. At last she went to rouse her husband, to see if he could not get rid of this tumult.

To her horror, Inary found that, although she shook her husband with all her might, she could not wake him. It was plain to see that he was bewitched by the Wee Folk.

Terrified by this, Inary left the fairies eating her last batch of bannocks and stole out of the house. She ran as fast as she could over the moor to the cottage of a certain wise man.

Inary knocked at his door until he put his head out of the window to see who was there.

The man listened in silence as Inary told him the whole story. Then he shook his head at her gravely.

"Let this be a lesson to you, foolish woman, never to pray for things that you do not need. Before your husband can be freed from the fairies' spell, you must get them out of the house and you must pour over him the fulling water in which they have boiled the wool.

"But first you must run to the top of the little hill behind your cottage. Some people call it Burg Hill; others call it the Fairie Knowe, for that is where the Little People live. There you must shout three times with all your might: '*Burg Hill is on fire!*'

"All the fairies will run out to see if it be true that their hill is burning. When they are out of your cottage, you must quickly bar the door and turn the kitchen topsy-turvy. You must upset everything that the fairies have worked with. If not, the things that their fingers have touched will open the door and let them in, in spite of you."

The housewife went away. She climbed to the top of the hill and three times cried with all her might: *"Burg Hill is on fire!"*

Almost before she had finished saying these words, the door of the cottage was flung wide open. All of the Little Folk came running out, knocking one another over in their eagerness to be home first at the hill. Each was calling for the things which he valued most and had left behind him in the Fairie Knowe.

Their cries sounded like this:

> *"Fetlock and cow*
> *Distaff and thread,*
> *Butter-kegs and cheese,*
> *My big meal chest;*
> *My sons and daughters,*
> *My wool cards and comb,*

My anvil and hammer,
My harrows and hoard;
My horses and traces,
My pigstys and pigs!
Burg Hill is on fire,
And if Burg Hill be burned
Our happy home
And merry life
Is gone."

While the Wee Folk were rushing and crying, the housewife slipped away down the back of the Knowe, and ran as fast as she could to her cottage. When she was once inside, it did not take her long to bar the door and turn everything upside down.

She took the band off the spinning wheel, and twisted the head of the distaff the opposite way. She lifted the pot of fulling water off the fire, turned the weaving loom topsy-turvy, and threw down the carding combs.

When she had done everything she could think

of, she put the griddle once more on the fire, and set to work to bake a griddleful of bannocks for her husband's breakfast, for the fairies had eaten up every bite of bread in the house.

She was busy at this when the Little Folk trooped back. They had soon found out that Burg Hill was not on fire at all.

"Good housewife, let us in," they cried as they knocked on the door.

"I cannot open the door," she answered, "for my hands are fast in the dough."

Then the fairies began to call to the things which their fingers had touched.

"Good Spinning Wheel, get up and open the door," they whispered.

"How can I?" answered the spinning wheel. "My band is undone."

"Kind Distaff! Open the door for us."

"That would I gladly do," said the distaff, "but I cannot walk, for my head is turned the wrong way."

"Weaving Loom! Have pity, and open the door."

"I am all topsy-turvy, and cannot help myself, far less help anyone else," sighed the loom.

"Pot of Fulling Water! Open the door," they implored.

"I am off the fire," growled the water, "and all my strength is gone."

The fairies became tired and impatient.

"Is there nothing that will come to our aid, and open the door?" they cried.

"I will," said a little barley bannock that was lying toasting on the hearth, and it rose and trundled quickly across the floor.

But, luckily, the housewife saw it. She nipped it between her finger and thumb, just as it was halfway across the kitchen. Because it was only half-baked, it fell with a *splatch* on the cold floor.

The fairies now gave up trying to enter the kitchen. Instead, they climbed through the windows into the room where the good housewife's husband was sleeping. They swarmed up on his bed, and ticked him until he became quite giddy. He talked nonsense and flung himself about, as if he had a fever.

What in the world shall I do now? said the housewife to herself. She wrung her hands in despair.

All of a sudden, she remembered what the wise man had said about the fulling water. She ran to the kitchen and lifted a cupful out of the pot. Back she rushed and threw it over her husband.

In an instant the husband woke up. Jumping out of bed, he ran across the room and opened the door. The fairies vanished, and they have never been seen there from that day to this.

Assipattle and the Giant Sea Serpent

LONG AGO in the north of Scotland there lived a well-to-do farmer. He and his goodwife had seven sons and one daughter.

The youngest son was called Assipattle, because he liked to lie before the fire wallowing in the ashes. His older brothers laughed at him and treated him with cuffs and kicks. They made him sweep the floor, bring in peats for the fire, and do any other little job too low for them.

Assipattle would have been unhappy but for

his sister, who loved him and was kind to him. She listened to his long stories about trolls and giants and encouraged him to tell more. His brothers, on the other hand, threw clods at him, and ordered him to stop his lying tales. What angered them most was that Assipattle himself was always the great hero in his tales.

One day something happened that made poor Assipattle very sad. A messenger came asking the farmer to send his pretty daughter to live in the King's house. She was to serve as maid to the beautiful Princess, who was the King's only child and much beloved.

Assipattle saw his sister go off, and he became silent and lonely.

After some time, another rider came by with the most terrible of tidings — that a giant sea serpent was drawing near the land. Hearing this, even the boldest hearts beat fast with fear.

True enough, a serpent came and turned his head toward the land. He opened his awful mouth and yawned horridly. And the noise of his jaws coming together again shook the earth and the sea. This he did to show that if he were not fed he would consume every living thing upon the land. He was well named the Master Sea Serpent — or the *Mester Stoorworm* — for he was the largest, the first and the father of all the sea serpents.

Fear fell upon every heart, and there was weeping in the land. The King summoned his council and they sat together for three days. But they could find no way to turn the monster away.

At last, when the council was at its wits' end, the Queen appeared. She was a bold woman, and stepmother to the King's beloved daughter.

Sternly she spoke to the councillors: "You are all brave men and great warriors — when you have only men to face. But now you deal with a foe that laughs at your strength. You must take counsel with the sorcerer, who knows all things. It is not by sword and spear, but by the wisdom

of sorcery that this monster can be overcome."

To this counsel the King and his men had to agree, although they disliked the sorcerer.

The sorcerer came in — a short and grisly man, looking like a goblin or bogle with his beard hanging down to his knees. He said that their question was a hard one, but he would give them counsel by sunrise.

Next day the sorcerer told the councillors that there was only one way to satisfy the sea serpent and to save the land. This was to feed the monster once a week with seven lovely lasses. "If this should not soon remove the monster," he said, "there will then be only one remedy — one so horrid that I must not mention it unless the first plan fails."

When people saw the serpent, they cried: "Is there no other way to save the land?"

Assipattle stared at the monster, and he was filled with rage and with pity. Suddenly he cried out: "Will no one fight the sea serpent and keep the lassies alive? I'm not afraid; I would fight the monster."

Everyone looked at Assipattle. "The poor bairn is mad," they said. His eldest brother gave him a kick and ordered him home to his ashes.

On their way home together, Assipattle persisted in saying that he would kill the monster. His brothers became so angry at what they thought was bragging that they pelted him with stones. Later, in the barn, they even tried to smother him with straw, but their father, coming by, saved him.

At supper, when their father objected to what the sons had done to their smaller brother, Assipattle answered: "You need not have come to my help. I could have fought them all. Aye, I could have beat every one of them had I wished."

They all laughed then and said: "Why did you not try?"

"Because I wanted to save my strength to fight the giant sea monster," said Assipattle.

Now over all the land there was weeping and wailing for the death of so many innocent lasses. If this went on, there would be no maidens left.

The council met again and called for the sorcerer. They demanded to know his second remedy.

The sorcerer raised his ugly head. "With cruel sorrow I say that the King's daughter herself must be given to the monster. Then only shall the monster leave our land."

The sorcerer pretended grief, but he knew it would please the Queen to be rid of the Princess.

A great silence filled the council chamber. At last the King arose — tall, grim and sorrowful. He said: "She is my only child. She is my dearest on earth. She should be my heir. Yet, if her death can save the land, let her die."

The councillors had to agree — but they did so in sorrow, for the Princess was beloved by everyone. When the head of the council, with sore heart, was about to pronounce the new edict, the

King's own guard, who had stood by him in many battles, now rose and said: "I ask that, if then the monster has not gone away, the sorcerer himself shall become the monster's next meal." The councillors gave such a shout of approval to this that the sorcerer paled and seemed to shrink.

The King asked for a delay of three weeks, so that he might make a proclamation. He would offer his daughter to any champion who would drive away the monster.

Messengers now rode to all the neighboring kingdoms, to announce that whosoever would, by war or craft, remove the sea serpent from the land should have the Princess for his wife. With her would be given also the kingdom — to which she was heir — and the King's famous sword, Sicker-snapper. That was the sword with which the great god Odin had fought his foes and driven them to the back side of the world. No man had any power against it.

Every young Prince and warrior was stirred by

the thought of a beautiful wife, a rich kingdom, and so great a sword. But, more than this, they were horrified by the edict that their beloved Princess was to be given to the monster unless someone drove it away.

Assipattle, hearing all this, sat among the ashes and said nothing.

Six-and-thirty champions rode to the King's palace, each one hoping to win the prize. But when they beheld the monster, lying out in the sea with his great mouth open, twelve of the number suddenly fell ill and were carried home. Twelve others were so terrified that they began to run away and never stopped till they reached their own lands. Only twelve stayed at the King's house, and these felt their hearts drop to their stomachs.

At the end of the three weeks, at evening before the great day when the Princess was to be sacrificed, the King gave a great supper. But it turned into a dreary feast; little was eaten, and less was said. There was no spirit of making fun, for everyone was thinking heavily of the morrow.

When all but the King and his faithful guard had gone to bed, the King opened the great seat on which he always sat. It was the high chair of state, and in it his most precious things were kept. He lifted out the great sword, Sickersnapper.

"Why take you out Sickersnapper?" asked the guard. "Your day for fighting is gone, my Lord. Let Sickersnapper lie, my good Lord. You are too old to wield her now."

"Wheest!" said the King in anger. "Or I'll try my sword on your body! Think you that I can see my only bairn devoured by a monster and not strike a blow for her? I tell you — and with my thumbs crossed on the edge of Sickersnapper I swear it — that I and this good sword both shall perish before my daughter die. And now, my trusty man, prepare my boat ready to sail, with her bow to sea. I will fight the serpent myself!"

At the farm that night the family made ready

to set out on the morrow to see what would happen on the great day. All were to go but Assipattle, who must stay home to herd the geese.

As Assipattle lay in his corner that night, he found he could not sleep. His mind was filling with plans. And he heard his parents talking. His mother said: "I do not think I will go with you tomorrow. I am not able to go so far on my feet and I do not care to ride alone." His father replied, "You need not ride alone. I'll take you behind me, on Swift-go. None will go so fast as we."

Next Assipattle heard his mother say to his father: "For the last five years I have begged you to tell me how it is that, with you, Swift-go outruns any other horse in the land, while if anyone else rides him he hobbles along like an old nag."

"Indeed, Goodwife," said the goodman, "I will not keep the secret from you longer. It is that when I want Swift-go to stand, I give him a clap on the left shoulder. When I want him to ride like any other horse, I give him two claps on the right. But when I want him to fly fast, I blow through the windpipe of a goose. To be ready at any time, I always keep the pipe in the right-hand pocket of my coat. When Swift-go hears that, he goes swift as a storm of wind. So, now you know all. Keep your mind at peace."

Assipattle lay quiet as a mouse till he heard the old folk snoring. But then he did not rest long. He pulled the goose's windpipe out of his father's pocket, and slipped away fast to the stable. Swiftly he bridled Swift-go and led him out.

Knowing he was not held by his own master, Swift-go pranced and reared madly. But Assi-

pattle remembered the secret and clapped his hand
on Swift-go's left shoulder, so that the horse stood
still as a stone. Assipattle jumped on his back, and
clapped his right shoulder. And away they went.

As they were leaving, the horse gave a loud,
loud neigh. This woke the farmer, who knew the
cry of his horse. He saw Swift-go vanishing in the
moonlight.

The farmer aroused his sons and they all
mounted and galloped after Swift-go, crying
"Thief!"

When Swift-go heard the farmer cry

> *"Hi, hi! ho!*
> *Swift-go, whoa!"*

he stopped for a moment. All would have been
lost had not Assipattle pulled out the goose's
windpipe. He blew through it with all his might.
Swift-go heard this and went off like the wind,
taking Assipattle swiftly beyond the others. The
farmer and his sons had to return home.

As day was dawning in the east, Assipattle saw the sea and lying in it the giant sea serpent he had come to slay. He could see the monster's tongue, jagged like a fork, with which it could sweep whatever it wanted into its mouth. But Assipattle had a hero's heart beneath his tattered rags — he was not afraid. I must be careful and do by my wits what I cannot manage by my strength, he thought.

Assipattle tethered his horse to a tree and walked till he came to a wee cottage. He found an old woman fast asleep in bed. He did not disturb her, but took down an old pot which he did not think she would mind his using to save the Princess's life. In the pot he placed a live peat from the fire.

Now, with pot and burning peat, he went to the shore. Near the water's edge he saw the King's boat with sails set and prow turned toward the monster. In the boat sat the man whose duty it was to watch till the King came.

"A nippy cold morning," said Assipattle to the man.

"Aye, it is that," said the man. "I have sat here all night till my very bones are frozen."

"Why don't you come on shore for a run, to warm yourself?" said Assipattle.

"Because," said the man, "if the King's guard found me out of the boat, he would half-kill me."

"Wise enough," says Assipattle. "You like a cold skin better than a hot. But I must kindle a fire to roast a few mussels, for hunger's like to eat a hole in my stomach."

With that, Assipattle began to dig a hole in which to make a fire. In a moment he cried out: "My stars! Gold! Gold! As sure as I am the son of my mother, there's gold in this earth!"

When the man in the boat heard this, he jumped to shore and pushed Assipattle roughly aside. And while the man scraped in the earth, Assipattle seized his pot, loosened the boat-rope, jumped into the boat, and pushed out to sea.

The outwitted man discovered what had happened and began to roar. And there was greater anger when the King arrived, carrying his great sword, Sickersnapper, in hopes of saving his daughter.

With the sun now peeping over the hills, the King and his company could only stand on shore and watch.

Assipattle had hoisted the sail and was steering for the head of the monster. The creature lay before him like an exceedingly big and high mountain, while the eyes of the monster glowed and flamed like a fire.

The sight might have terrified the bravest heart.

The monster's length stretched half across the world and his tongue was hundreds and hundreds of miles long. When in anger, he could with his tongue sweep whole towns, trees, and hills into the sea. His terrible tongue was forked, and he used the prongs as a pair of tongs with which to seize his prey. With that fork he could crush the largest ship like an eggshell. He could crack the walls of the biggest castle like a nut, and suck every living thing out of the castle into his mouth. Still, Assipattle had no fear.

Assipattle sailed up to the side of the serpent's head. Then, taking down his sail, he lay quietly on his oars, thinking his own thoughts. When the sun struck the monster's eyes, it gave a hideous yawn — the first of seven that it yawned before its awful breakfast. Each time the monster yawned, a great tide of sea water rushed down its throat and came out again through its huge gills.

Assipattle rowed close to the monster's head,

with his sails down. At the second yawn, he and the boat were sucked in by the inrushing tide. But the boat did not stay in the monster's mouth. The tide carried her on, down a black throat that yawned like a bottomless pit. It was not very dark for Assipattle, for the roof and sides of the tunnel were covered with a substance from the sea which gave a soft, silvery light in the creature's throat. On and on, down and down, went Assipattle. He steered his boat in midstream. As he went down, the water became more shallow, with part of it going out through the gills. The top of the tunnel began to get lower, till the boat's mast stuck its end in the roof, and her keel stuck on the bottom of the throat.

Assipattle now jumped out. Pot in hand, he waded and ran, and began to explore, till he came to the monster's enormous liver. He cut a hole in the liver, and placed in it his live peat. He blew and blew on the burning peat till he thought his lips would crack. At length the peat began to flame. The flame caught the oil of the liver, and in a minute there was a large, hot fire.

Assipattle ran back to the boat as fast as his feet could carry him. When the serpent felt the heat of the fire, he began to cough. There arose terrible floods. One of these caught the boat and flung it, with Assipattle, right out — high and dry on the shore.

The King and all the people drew back to a high hill, where they were safe from the floods sent out by the monster. The serpent was indeed a terrible sight. After the floods of water, there came from its mouth and nose great clouds of smoke black as pitch. As the fire grew within the monster, it flung out its awful tongue and waved it to and fro until its end reached up and struck the moon. When the tongue fell back on the earth, it was so sudden and violent a fall that it cut the earth and made a long length of sea where there had been dry land. That is the sea that now divides Denmark from Sweden and Norway.

Now the serpent drew in his long tongue, and

his struggles and twisting were a terror to behold. The fiery pain made him fling up his head to the clouds. As his head fell back, the force of the fall knocked out a number of his teeth, and these teeth became the Orkney Islands. Again his head rose and fell, and he shed more of his teeth. These became the Shetland Islands. Finally the serpent coiled himself up into a great lump, and died. That lump became Iceland. And the fire that Assipattle kindled still burns in the mountains there.

And now everyone could plainly see that the monster was dead. The King took Assipattle in his arms and kissed him and blessed him and called him his son. He took off his own mantle and put it on Assipattle. And he girded on him the great sword, Sickersnapper. He took the Princess's hand and put it in Assipattle's hand, and he said that when the right time came the two should be married and Assipattle would rule over all the kingdom.

Assipattle mounted Swift-go and rode by the

Princess's side. The whole company mounted their horses and returned with joy to the castle, where Assipattle's sister came running out to meet them.

Assipattle's sister told the King that the Queen and the sorcerer had fled on the two best horses in the stable. "They'll ride fast if I don't find them," said Assipattle. And with that, he went off like the wind on Swift-go, and soon caught up with the two. When the sorcerer saw Assipattle come so near, he said to the Queen: "It's only some boy. I'll cut off his head at once." But Assipattle drew Sickersnapper, and with one dread thrust drove the sword through the sorcerer's heart. As for the Queen, she was brought back and made prisoner in a castle tower.

When Assipattle and the Princess were married there was a wedding feast that lasted nine weeks, as jolly as a feast in Yule. They became King and Queen and lived in joy and splendor. And, if not dead, they are yet alive.